Dear Parent:
Your child's love of reading starts here!

Every child learns to read in a different way and at his or her own speed. Some go back and forth between reading levels and read favorite books again and again. Others read through each level in order. You can help your young reader improve and become more confident by encouraging his or her own interests and abilities. From books your child reads with you to the first books he or she reads alone, there are I Can Read Books for every stage of reading:

SHARED READING
Basic language, word repetition, and whimsical illustrations, ideal for sharing with your emergent reader

BEGINNING READING
Short sentences, familiar words, and simple concepts for children eager to read on their own

READING WITH HELP
Engaging stories, longer sentences, and language play for developing readers

READING ALONE
Complex plots, challenging vocabulary, and high-interest topics for the independent reader

ADVANCED READING
Short paragraphs, chapters, and exciting themes for the perfect bridge to chapter books

I Can Read Books have introduced children to the joy of reading since 1957. Featuring award-winning authors and illustrators and a fabulous cast of beloved characters, I Can Read Books set the standard for beginning readers.

A lifetime of discovery begins with the magical words "I Can Read!"

Visit www.icanread.com for information
on enriching your child's reading experience.

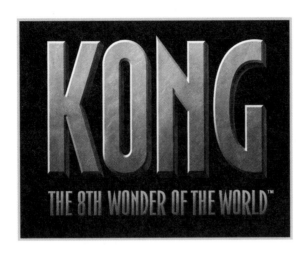

JOURNEY TO
SKULL
ISLAND

King Kong: Journey to Skull Island

© 2005 Universal Studios Licensing LLLP. Universal Studios' King Kong movie © Universal Studios. Kong The 8th Wonder of the World™ Universal Studios. All Rights Reserved. No part of this book may be used or reproduced in any manner whatsoever without written permission except in the case of brief quotations embodied in critical articles and reviews. Printed in the United States of America. For information address HarperCollins Children's Books, a division of HarperCollins Publishers, 1350 Avenue of the Americas, New York, NY 10019. www.harperchildrens.com

Library of Congress Catalog Card Number: 2005928976
ISBN-10: 0-06-077299-9 (pbk.) — ISBN-13: 978-0-06-077299-4 (pbk.)

4   5   6   7   8   9   10   ❖   First Edition

I Can Read!

READING 2 WITH HELP

KONG
THE 8TH WONDER OF THE WORLD™

JOURNEY TO
SKULL
ISLAND

Adapted by Jennifer Frantz

Illustrations by Peter Bollinger and
Robert Papp

Based on a Motion Picture Screenplay by
Fran Walsh & Philippa Boyens &
Peter Jackson

Based on a story by Merian C. Cooper and
Edgar Wallace

HarperCollins*Publishers*

Far across the open sea

lies a mysterious island.

It is not found on most maps,

and no one ever visits.

It is called Skull Island.

Skull Island is always surrounded
by a thick curtain of fog.
Pass through the fog and land upon
Skull Island's sinking shores—
if you dare.

Stepping ashore from your boat,
you will feel a tingle down your spine.
Your senses spring to life.

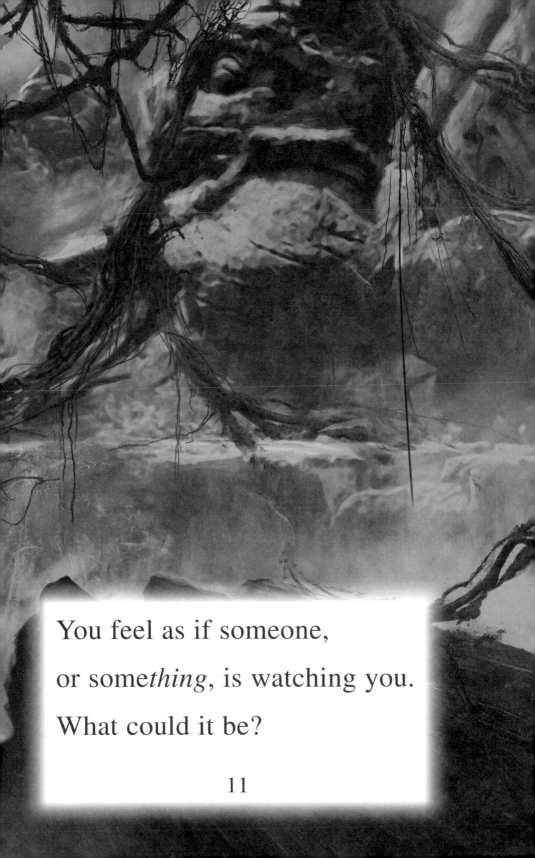

You feel as if someone,

or some*thing*, is watching you.

What could it be?

Travel farther and you will find a giant wall lined with spikes and torches.

The wall keeps danger out.

If you are brave, you may venture beyond the wall.

There lies a dense jungle. It has plants so thick you cannot see through them.

14

Listen closely and you will hear leaves rustling and twigs snapping behind you. . . .

Is something following you?

Look out!

A huge dinosaur with razor-sharp teeth snaps its powerful jaws.

Another whips its spiky tail.

Others pound their giant feet
on the rocky ground.

Skull Island should have sunk
beneath the sea long, long ago.
But it survived.
It is full of prehistoric creatures,
like dinosaurs, and insects as big
as people.

But those are not the only creatures that live on Skull Island.

Press on ahead to find out more.

Through the jungle lies a body of water.

It is a dark and murky swamp.

20

It is a place filled with danger.

What is that in the water?

Rising from the shadowy depths,

a water serpent rears up as tall as

a house.

Move quickly now.

You are getting closer—

closer to the true secret
of Skull Island.

In the distance, a great mountain appears.

Your heart begins to beat faster as you look up at it.

Atop the mountain
there is a huge cave—
a rocky lair.
Giant bats are swarming.

Suddenly you feel the ground shake.

A loud roar fills the air.

ROAR!

You can almost feel the hot breath

of the creature who made it.

Then he appears.

The eighth wonder of the world.

There he is—Kong!

Looking over his island,

Kong pounds his massive chest.

He throws back his head

and lets out another deafening roar.

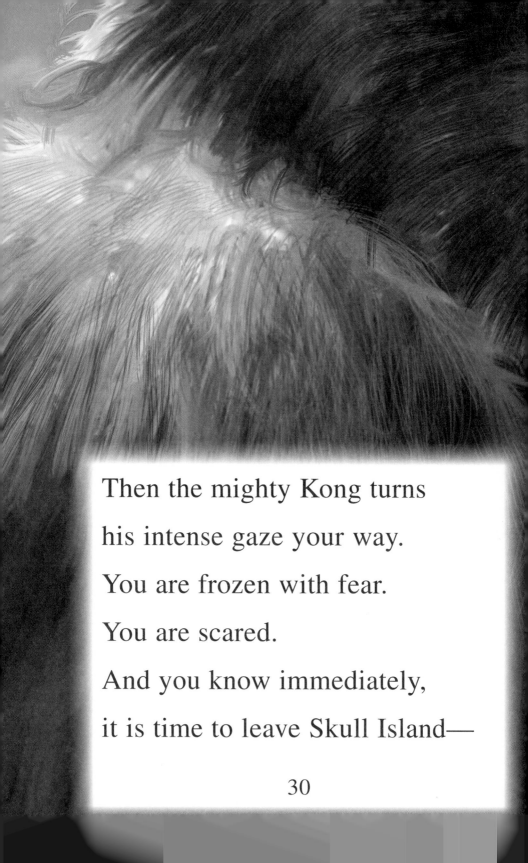

Then the mighty Kong turns

his intense gaze your way.

You are frozen with fear.

You are scared.

And you know immediately,

it is time to leave Skull Island—

30

while you still can!

You run away quickly, back to
your boat and to safety.

31

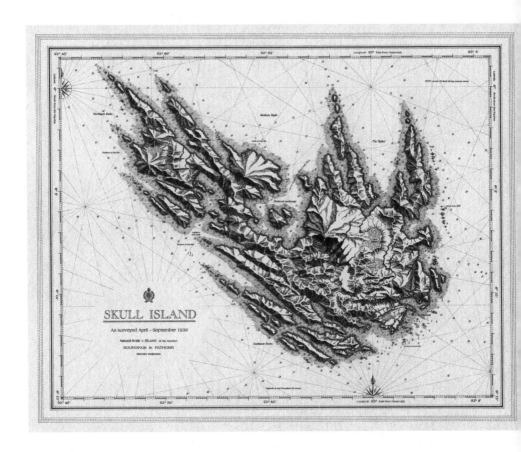

Now you know the secret of
Skull Island.
You have seen the beast named
Kong and made it out safely.
But are you brave enough to ever
return?